★ TODAY'S ★
HEROES
Ben Carson

Other books in the Today's Heroes Series

★ TODAY'S ★ HEROES
Ben Carson

Gregg & Deborah Shaw Lewis

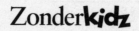

Today's Heroes: Ben Carson
Copyright © 2002 by Gregg and Deborah Shaw Lewis

Requests for information should be addressed to:

Zonder**kidz**™

The children's group of Zondervan

Grand Rapids, Michigan 49530
www.zonderkidz.com

ISBN: 0-310-70298-4

Photography © Vic Raspa
Cover Design: Lookout Design Group
Interior design by Todd Sprague
Printed in the United States of America

03 04 05 06 07 / DC/ 10 9 8

CONTENTS

THE DUMBEST KID IN FIFTH GRADE

Hey, Dummy!"

Ben Carson looked up. "Dummy" was the nickname his classmates had given him.

Another fifth grader laughed at Ben's instinctive response: "Ben Carson is *so* dumb."

Ben shrugged and tried to act as if he didn't mind. He didn't like being called dumb. Who would? But he figured what the kid said was true. After all, he heard it every single day.

"Ben Carson's the dumbest kid in fifth grade!" the kid continued.

Ben looked the other way. He wasn't in the mood to argue.

"Hey, Carson's the dumbest kid in the world!" someone else called out.

Now wait a minute! Ben thought. *I know I'm dumb. I have plenty of test grades to prove that. But surely somewhere in the world there has to be someone dumber than I am!*

It was time to draw the line. "I'm *not* the dumbest kid in the world!"

"You are too!"

"I am not!" Ben insisted.

"Couldn't be anybody in the world dumber than you are, Carson!"

The two argued back and forth until the teacher called the class inside.

Later that same afternoon, there was a math quiz. Afterward, the teacher had each student pass his test to the person behind him to correct as the teacher read out the answers. Ben knew what was coming next. Each student would have to report his or her score to the teacher—out loud!

Ben stared with disgust at the big fat zero on the top of his paper. *This oughta be good*, he thought. *When everybody finds out what I made on this quiz, they'll never let up.*

That's when Ben began to scheme: *Maybe if I mumble*, he thought, *the teacher won't understand me.* So when the teacher called his name, he muttered, "Nnme." And it worked!

"Nine! Benjamin? How wonderful! Class, can you see what Benjamin has done? Didn't I tell you if you just applied yourself you could do it? I'm so proud of you!"

Nine right meant Ben had twenty-one wrong, but nine was still a lot better than his usual grade. That must have been why the teacher just kept raving on . . . at least until the girl who had graded Ben's paper decided to set the record straight.

"He said *none*," she spouted. "You know, *none*—as in *not any*!"

After a short pause, a chorus of laughter broke out around the room, and the teacher just shook her head as she sat down in her chair. Ben wanted to disappear into thin air. But he couldn't. So he just smiled and tried to pretend that the laughter didn't bother him.

A few weeks later, Ben peeked at his midterm grade report. He was not surprised to see that he had failed most of his subjects. His brother Curtis received a report that wasn't much better. When Ben got home, he dropped his grade card along with his books on the table, hoping his mother wouldn't see them until after he was in bed.

No such luck. His mother picked up his grade card and looked it over carefully. "Bennie, is this your midterm report?" she finally asked.

"Yes, ma'am," Ben replied, "but it doesn't mean much."

"No, Bennie," she answered, "it means a lot! If you keep making grades like this, you'll spend the rest of your life sweeping floors in a factory. And that's not what God wants for you!"

His mom pulled Ben and Curtis close to her and looked right into their faces. "Boys, I don't know what to do. But God promises in the Bible to give wisdom to those who ask. So tonight I'm going to pray for wisdom. I am going to ask God what I need to do to help you."

Ben and Curtis didn't know what to think about their mother's words. Had she gone off the deep end? Did she really think God was going to tell her how to help them get better grades?

Two days later, the boys found out how God intended to answer their mother's prayer, and they didn't like it. "God says we need to turn off the television," Mrs. Carson told her sons. "You may choose two TV shows to watch each week. We'll spend the rest of the time reading."

The boys tried to object, but their mother wasn't finished. "You are also to write two book reports every week about the books you read. Then you can read your reports out loud to me."

God's answer didn't seem very wise to Ben and Curtis. But they did what their mother asked them to do. They turned off the television, walked to the nearest branch of the Detroit Public Library, and checked out a stack of books.

The boys were grateful that their mother hadn't said *what* they had to read. That meant they were free to choose books they were interested in. Ben loved animals. So he read all the animal books he could find and then moved on to plants and rocks.

The Carsons lived in a section of Detroit near some railroad tracks. Soon, Ben found himself collecting rocks in little boxes and taking them home to look up in his library books. Before long, he could identify almost any rock he found. He was proud of himself, but he thought it wise not to mention his new hobby to anyone at school.

One day Mr. Jaeck, Ben's science teacher, walked into his fifth-grade classroom with a big shiny black rock. He held it up and asked, "Can anyone tell me what this is?"

Ben waited for one of the smart kids to answer. No one did. So he waited for one of the dumb kids to respond. No one did. Finally, his hand went up. And as it did, his classmates began to whisper and giggle. "Hey, look, Carson has his hand up! This oughta be good!"

Mr. Jaeck was surprised too. "Benjamin?"

"That's obsidian." Ben answered. Suddenly, the classroom was quiet. It sounded good. But no one was sure if it was the right answer—or a joke.

"That's right. It *is* obsidian," Mr. Jaeck exclaimed.

No one else was saying anything, so Ben continued, "Obsidian is formed after a volcanic eruption. Lava flows down and when it hits water, there is a super-cooling process. The elements mix together, forcing out the air. Then the surface glazes—

"Right again, Benjamin," Mr. Jaeck remarked with excitement in his voice. "Class, this is a tremendous piece of information Benjamin has just given us! I'm proud of him." Before he went on with his lesson, Mr. Jaeck asked Ben to stop by after school and work on his rock collection with him.

Everyone was staring at Ben in astonishment. But the most surprised person in the room was Ben himself. For the first time, he realized that he was not such a dummy after all!

Ben also realized that he'd known the answer because he'd been reading books. As that sank in, he began to wonder, *What if I read books about all my subjects? Maybe I would know more than anyone in the class—more than the kids who tease me and call me names!*

Ben had made a giant discovery. But he couldn't yet imagine how much reading would change his life. He had found the key that would unlock his future and someday enable his greatest dreams to come true.

2

A MISSIONARY DOCTOR

There had been a time a few years earlier when Ben felt his dreams could never come true.

When Ben was eight years old and his brother, Curtis, was ten, they lived with their father and mother in Detroit, Michigan. For a long time, Ben had sensed that something was wrong. It wasn't that he heard his parents scream and shout at each other. He seldom even heard them argue. Instead they would quit talking to each other until the whole house filled with a deep and disturbing quiet.

Those silences gradually became longer and much more frequent. His father seemed to be gone more and more. But Ben was still surprised when his mother announced that his father would not be living with them anymore.

At first he wondered if he'd done something to make his father angry. But his mother assured him that his father loved him very much and was not mad at him at all. Still, it hurt.

"I don't want him to leave!" Ben had cried. "Please make him come back!"

But Ben's mother simply shook her head and said she was sorry. "Bennie, your father can't come back. He's done some . . . some bad things." And that was as much as she would tell Ben and Curtis.

Ben argued and argued with his mother. "If he did something wrong, why can't you just forgive him and let him come home?" Ben's heart was broken. He loved his daddy.

Every night he prayed for his father to come home so their family could be together again. But he never did.

What Ben couldn't understand at the time, and didn't know until he was much older, was that his father was a bigamist. When Ben's father had told them he had to be away from home traveling for his job, he was lying. The truth was that Ben's father had another wife and family living in another city. He had been living a lie for many years.

Even after Ben learned the truth, he continued to love his father in spite of what he had done. But Ben loved and respected his mother even more. He knew how hard she had to work to take care of him and Curtis and how hard it must have been for her to accept his father's actions.

Sonya Carson had been born into a large and extremely poor rural Tennessee family. She was the next to the youngest of twenty-four children. But she knew only thirteen of her siblings because she spent most of her lonely and unhappy childhood moving from one foster home to another.

She had been only thirteen years old when she met and married Ben's father, an older man who promised to rescue her from her sad life and take her north to Detroit. He promised to provide her with a life of wealth and adventure. Ben's father was a charming man and a good provider. He loved parties and seemed proud of his young wife. He often bought Ben's mother expensive gifts of clothing and jewelry. But with time, Ben's mother became concerned about their finances. Ben's father seemed to spend money as fast as he earned it.

After the boys were born, Ben's mother wondered where her husband was getting his extra money. She worried that he might be involved in selling alcohol or even drugs.

She finally found out that he had another wife and family, and she told him to leave.

When he left, Ben's father took all of the family's money. Ben's mother had no job skills or work experience, so she supported herself and her two sons by cleaning houses and taking care of children. It was hard work, but she was determined to do whatever it took to provide for her boys.

Ben found it tough to give up his dream of a happy home where his family could all live together again. But the same year his father left, a new dream entered Ben's life—a dream that made the reality of his family situation a little easier to live with.

Ben's dream was born one Sunday morning during church. Ben sat on the edge of the pew, listening carefully as their minister told an exciting true story about a missionary doctor.

"Robbers were chasing the doctor and his wife," the minister told them. "They ran as fast as they could around trees and over rocks, trying to stay ahead of their pursuers. Then they came to the edge of a cliff. They had nowhere to go. Then, right at the very edge of the cliff, they spotted a crack in the rock just big enough for both of them to crawl into.

"When the bandits got to the cliff, their would-be victims were nowhere to be seen. It was as if the doctor and his wife had vanished! The robbers didn't know what to think! They stomped around cursing and then left. The missionaries were safe."

As the story ended, Ben breathed a sigh of relief. What a thrilling life missionaries must lead!

"God hid his missionaries in the cleft of the rock," the pastor explained. "And he will do the same for you if you give him your heart and let him protect you from harm."

That's what I need, thought Ben. So when the preacher asked those who wanted to meet Jesus to come to the front of the sanctuary, Ben got up and walked down the aisle to where the minister was standing. After listening to that exciting story, Ben knew two things: he knew he wanted Jesus to watch over him, and he knew what he wanted to do with his life.

"I know what I want to do when I grow up," Ben told his mother as they walked home from church that day. "I want to be a missionary doctor."

His mother stopped and looked right at him. "Bennie," she said, "if you ask the Lord for something and believe that he will do it, it will happen."

His mother's response only confirmed the dream for him. From that time on, Ben was convinced that God wanted him to be a doctor one day. Somehow he held on to that dream despite a lot of other difficult and unhappy things that happened in his young life.

★

Since Ben's father was not giving them any money, his mother had to work longer and longer hours, holding two or three jobs at a time. For a few months, they were able to stay in their house in Detroit. Then, to save money, Ben's mother decided to move her little family to Boston, Massachusetts, where they could live with Ben's Aunt Jean. Ben's mother told the boys that they would rent out their house in Detroit for enough money to pay the monthly mortgage payments. That way, when times were better, they could move back into their home on Deacon Street.

Ben was sad about leaving his home and friends in Michigan to live in a tenement building in Boston.

It wasn't until later that Ben found out there was something good about living with Aunt Jean and Uncle William. Their children were grown, and they had lots of love to show two young boys. The first Christmas they lived in Boston, his aunt, uncle, and mother showered the boys with gifts.

Ben's favorite gift was a chemistry set. He spent hours in his room, reading the instructions and mixing chemicals and watching them react. One of his experiments left the apartment smelling like rotten eggs. Ben thought that was so funny that he laughed and laughed.

The worst part of living in Boston was the rats that roamed in packs in the weeds behind the tenement house where they now lived. Big rats. Ugly rodents as big as cats. Lots of them. The horrid creatures usually stayed away from the building. But in cold weather, they sometimes took refuge in the basement.

Once, a big snake slithered into the basement of their building. Someone killed it. But afterward, the neighborhood kids told stories about snakes eating children. Between the rats he'd seen and the snakes he heard about, Ben was always afraid to go into the basement.

Ben's mother worked for several families, caring for their children or cleaning their houses.

Many days she left for work early in the morning before her boys went to school and didn't get home until almost bedtime. Just the same, she always took time to ask Ben and Curtis what they were doing and learning in school. Always. No matter how tired she was or how many hours she had worked that day. Ben and his brother knew their mother thought their education was important and that she wanted them to excel in school. And they did. Both boys were doing well in their classes at the small private school they attended in Boston.

Ben's mother wanted her sons to learn the importance of setting goals in life. So almost every day, she talked to Ben and Curtis about her goal to move back into their house in Detroit.

Sonya Carson also taught her sons the value of a dollar. For instance, riding to school on the city bus cost twenty cents a day—the price of a loaf of bread then. So Ben and Curtis rode their bikes to school, and the money they saved was used to buy groceries for the family.

Ben's mother liked to say, "A penny saved is a penny earned." So the boys learned never to return a book to the library even one day late to avoid the two-cent fine. They never walked past an alley without looking to see if they could spot a bottle they could turn in for a penny deposit. No amount of money was too small when it came to spending—or saving.

★

In two years, the Carson family had saved enough pennies, nickels, and dimes to move back to Detroit. They still couldn't afford to move back into the house on Deacon Street. But they were closer. And the boys were glad to be back near old friends.

A few weeks after they went back to school in Detroit, both Ben and Curtis learned they had a serious problem. Instead of being among the better students as they had been in their classes in Boston, they found they were among the poorer students. Ben understood so little of what his class was studying that he began to believe what the other kids were saying about him, that he was dumb, and he feared his dream of becoming a missionary doctor was drifting out of reach.

3

BRAINS, TRAINS, AND RACIAL INJUSTICE

Ben felt especially dumb one day at Higgins Elementary when he couldn't read the letters on an eye chart. All students in fifth grade had to have their eyes tested. The boy ahead of Ben rattled off the letters and numbers easily. When Ben's turn came, he squinted and tried, but he couldn't make out any of the letters except for the very top line.

He was so embarrassed! He couldn't even get an eye chart right! "No wonder the kids call me 'Dummy,'" he mumbled.

Then the nurse giving the test told Ben that not being able to read the chart had nothing to do with being smart or dumb. He just needed glasses. The doctor who fitted Ben with glasses told him, "Your vision is so bad, you almost qualify as handicapped!"

When he wore his new glasses to school, Ben couldn't believe the difference. He could actually read what the teacher wrote on the board. Even from the back of the room.

Those new glasses were only the beginning. It was right after Ben got his glasses that Mrs. Carson asked God for wisdom and decided Ben and Curtis needed to read those two books a week and write book reports for her.

Some people thought Ben's mother was being too hard on her sons. Several of her friends talked to her, telling her that her boys needed more time to play outside. They warned her that Curtis and Ben would hate her for making them turn off the television to read books and write reports.

But they were wrong. Ben never hated his mother. Yes, he told her she was making them work too hard. But inside he knew that she loved him and Curtis and only wanted the best for them. He believed her when she told him that if he tried, he could do whatever he wanted to do.

Ben's mother was tough and demanding. One day Ben was riding in the car with his mother when the traffic stopped suddenly and another car bumped their car from behind. Without even getting out of his car to see how much damage he had caused, the man quickly drove away. Ben's mom chased him all the way across Detroit before he finally gave up, pulled over, and got out to give Mrs. Carson his insurance information.

Sonya Carson was just as tough and demanding with her sons. She had high expectations for

Curtis and Ben, and she never let them forget it. She observed the lives and habits of the successful and wealthy people whose homes she cleaned every day. "They're no different from us," she told her sons. "Anything they can do, you can do. And you can do it better."

In her mind, education was the key to her sons' success. And when other parents questioned the demands she placed on Curtis and Ben, she would tell them, "Say what you want, but my boys are going to be something. They're going to be self-supporting and learn how to love other folks. And no matter what they decide to do, they're going to be the best in the world at it."

★

The last week of fifth grade, Ben's class had a spelling bee. Just as everyone expected, the winner was Bobby Farmer. But what really surprised Ben was the word that Bobby had to spell in order to win the spelling bee—"agriculture."

I can spell that word! Ben thought. He had read it just the night before in one of his books. *If I can spell that word, I can learn to spell better than Bobby Farmer.*

That day Ben Carson made up his mind to keep on reading until he was the smartest kid in his class—just like his mother said he could be. He began to read whenever and wherever he could. He read before school and after school. He read when he was in the bathroom. He read books when he was waiting for the bus. He kept on reading until, less than two years later, he had gone from the "dumbest kid in fifth grade" to the top of his seventh-grade class at Wilson Junior High School. The same students who had laughed at him on the playground that day back in the fifth grade now came to him and asked for his help with their schoolwork.

Ben liked that. He enjoyed having other students come to him for help. It made him proud to know that he had earned their respect.

★

Like most African-American kids, Ben and Curtis encountered racial injustice, but perhaps not as much as a lot of other black kids their ages. Their mother tried to shield them from it. For most of their lives, the boys had lived in black neighborhoods, attended black schools, and worshiped in black churches. So it wasn't until the Carsons moved back to Detroit from Boston and Ben enrolled in Higgins Elementary that he encountered racism.

One student in Ben's fifth-grade class, a white boy named John, had done such an outstanding job on a class science project that he had been given the honor of representing the entire school on a television science program broadcast into schools around the state three days a week.

The entire fifth grade watched eagerly on the day their classmate was scheduled to appear. Ben was sitting next to a girl named Christine when the two of them got into a guessing game as to just when John's turn would come. So when one segment of the show ended, in an attempt to be the first one to guess, Ben blurted out, "John will be next!"

When a black student walked out on the set instead, some of the kids snickered. And Christine actually leaned over to punch Ben and announced, "I should ring your neck," as if Ben had implied that John, the pride of Higgins Elementary School, was "colored." In that moment, Ben felt a terrible sinking, sick feeling in the pit of his stomach. He suddenly realized that Christine, and evidently the rest of his white classmates, considered it an unthinkable insult to be black.

Later that same year, Ben experienced another racist incident. One day after school, Ben was playing with some white children out on the street when an angry shout called them into the house. Ben was walking away when one of the kids sneaked back out and caught up with him. "We can't play with you anymore," the child said, "cause you're a 'blackie.'" Ben was beginning to understand that being black was not a good thing to many people.

At the junior high school, like at Higgins Elementary, most of the students were white. There, too, Ben encountered prejudice.

Railroad tracks ran alongside the route that Ben and his brother took to Wilson Junior High. So for the excitement of it, they began hopping trains on their way to school. Curtis would toss his clarinet onto one flat car, then jump and catch the railing on the last car on the train. Curtis liked to catch the faster trains. Ben watched for the slower-moving trains. But both boys were placing themselves in great danger. Not only did they have to jump, catch the railing, and hold on, but they also had to watch out for railroad security men, who were always on the lookout for people hopping the trains.

The security guards never caught Ben and Curtis. But one day when Ben was alone, he got caught by a group of bigger boys, all of them white. One was carrying a big stick.

The boy with the stick hit Ben across his shoulders, and the others all crowded around. Ben had nowhere to go. The boys yelled and called Ben ugly names.

Ben was small and skinny for his age. He knew he was no match for even one of these boys. He knew he couldn't defend himself, so he just stared at the ground.

"If we ever catch you again, we'll kill you!" the boy yelled before letting Ben go. Ben ran all the way to school and never hopped a train again.

Later that same year, Ben and Curtis went out for the football team. Neither Carson boy was big, but they were fast. Both did well in football until one day a group of young, angry white men surrounded them as they were leaving practice. Ben and Curtis were frightened. Finally, one of the white men stepped forward and said, "You two ever come back, and we'll throw you in the river!"

Ben and Curtis never found out if the young men would have actually hurt them because they never went back to football practice.

Ben's worst encounter with racial prejudice took place in a school assembly. What made it so bad was that the prejudice came from one of his teachers.

The teacher called Ben to the front of the auditorium to receive the award for the highest academic achievement in his grade. After handing him the award, she turned back to the microphone and tried to shame the white kids for letting a black kid beat them. "You are not trying hard enough!" she told them. Her message was clear: she thought white kids were smarter than black kids and that no black student should have been number one.

Several of Ben's white friends looked at him and rolled their eyes as if to say, "Isn't she dumb!"

Ben wondered what was wrong with the teacher. He had been in her class. She knew how hard he worked and how smart he was. He had earned this award! Ben was angry, but he didn't show it.

By ninth grade, racism no longer came as a shock to Ben, though it still hurt and infuriated him. The last day of his first term in high school, Ben had to carry his report card around from class to class so that each teacher could fill in the grade for that course. Ben had straight A's in every subject going into his last class of the day—physical education. His gym teacher, who was white, looked over all of his grades, and then looked up at Ben. Ben had earned an A in the class, but the teacher wrote in a B—and then looked up and grinned. The teacher knew he had ruined Ben's chance to make the A honor roll. He also knew there was nothing Ben could do about it.

Ben never told his mother what the PE teacher had done. He never told her about the kids by the train tracks. Or what the teacher had said at the honors assembly. And neither he nor Curtis ever told her the real reason they quit playing football. They didn't want their mother to worry about them.

4

A CHANGE AND NOT FOR THE BETTER

Halfway through Ben's eighth-grade year, the Carsons moved back into their old house on Deacon Street. His mother had finally reached her goal. The house was small, but it felt like home!

To Ben, it was a dream come true. But it meant changing schools once again. Leaving his friends at Wilson Junior High, he became the "new kid" at Hunter Junior High. Ben was still one of the brightest kids in his class. But unlike the students at Wilson, his new classmates didn't seem to care about who *was* smart.

They cared more about who *dressed* smart. And the smart clothes, the "in" look, was expensive: Italian knit shirts, silk pants, alligator shoes, and stingy brim hats. Ben's mother had no money for such things.

At Wilson, the other students had respected Ben because of his intelligence. To be respected at Hunter, you had to dress right, play basketball, and learn how to "cap" people. Capping meant to say something funny—but critical—about another person, to get the better of someone.

His first few weeks at Hunter Junior High, Ben quickly became a favorite target for the other boys to "cap" on. He was new and his clothes were definitely not "in."

"Know what the Indians did with General Custer's worn-out clothes?" one boy asked.

"Tell us!" another one exclaimed.

"They saved them for our man Carson here!" came the response.

"Sure looks it," a third boy chimed in.

"Get close enough and you'll believe it, 'cuz they smell like they are a hundred years old," the first boy said to finish off the "capping."

For several weeks, Ben took this abuse quietly. He didn't know what to do to make friends with his new classmates. *What's wrong with me?* Ben wondered. *Why do I have to be different?*

Then he decided that the best way to survive capping was to become the best capper. Ben thought, *You guys want to cap? I can show you how to cap!*

The next day, Ben was ready. A ninth grader started it.

"Man, that shirt you're wearing has been through World War I, World War II, World War III, and World War IV!"

"Yeah," Ben answered, "and your mama wore it!"

The students standing around all laughed—even the boy who had started the capping. He slapped Ben on the back and said, "Hey, that's okay!"

It didn't take long for the crowd who had been picking on Ben to direct their attention elsewhere. They knew if they started capping on Ben, he could top their remarks. Ben was glad.

But he still didn't fit in at his new school. The kids at Hunter seemed to think that if you were poor, you were worthless.

And Ben knew that his family was still poor even though they were back in their own house. Ben's family received food stamps from the government. Without that help, Ben's mother would not have been able to pay the other bills.

But Ben didn't want anyone to know that his family used food stamps. When he went to the grocery store to buy milk or bread, he would watch the checkout area carefully to be sure that no one from school saw him buy food with the food stamps. If someone walked in while he was standing in line, he would pretend he had forgotten something and walk to the back of the store until the coast was clear. Every time he left his house with food stamps in his pocket, he was afraid that someone would see him use them, and they would then know that he was poor.

By the time Ben was in the tenth grade, he thought his clothes were his biggest problem in life. More than anything, he wanted to dress like the "in" group at school. And he argued with his mother about it.

"Bennie," his mother said, "what you wear doesn't make any difference."

"But everyone will laugh at me!" Ben would respond.

"Only stupid people laugh at someone because of the clothes he wears," his mother would answer. "Just because someone dresses better than you, that doesn't make them better."

Almost every day Ben begged his mother for better clothes. Ben knew they couldn't afford them and that he was disappointing his mother, but he wanted desperately to be a part of the "in" crowd.

Instead of coming home from school and doing his homework, Ben started staying out, playing basketball, and hanging out with friends. Soon his grades slipped from A's to B's and then to C's.

Even though he became one of the gang because of his poor grades, the popular crowd still didn't accept him. He didn't wear the right clothes. Ben wanted so badly to be "cool" that he complained more and more to his mother. He begged her to buy him an Italian knit shirt—if nothing else. Ben's mother let him know how disappointed she was to hear what he was saying. After all, she thought she'd raised him to be different—not the kind of person who always has to do the same things everyone else is doing. She told him she thought he was too smart to fall for the latest fad and just follow along with people who aren't using their brains.

But Ben told her all he was asking for—all it would take to make him happy—was one Italian knit shirt. That's when his mother made him a deal. "Okay, I'll bring home all the money I make next week and turn it over to you, Ben. You'll be in charge of all the family finances. You can buy all the groceries, pay the bills, and take care of all the necessities. Whatever you have left over at the end of the week is yours. You can spend it on Italian knit shirts or whatever else you want."

This is going to be great! Ben thought. He bought the groceries and then began going through the other bills. But he ran out of money long before everything had been paid.

He suddenly realized that his mother, with her third-grade education, was some kind of genius just to keep food on the table and any kind of clothes on his back. He'd been complaining and asking her to buy him a $75 shirt when she brought home only $100 a week, working her fingers to the bone, scrubbing other people's floors and cleaning other people's toilets.

How could I have been so selfish? he thought.

Ben started studying again, and his grades went back up to A's. Some of his classmates laughed and called him "nerd" and "Poindexter," but he was determined not to let that bother him anymore.

Besides, he could always shut up his teasers and tormentors by saying one thing: "Let's see what I'm doing in twenty years, and then let's see what you're doing in twenty years." Ben not only had a dream, he had a plan for getting there. And the people around him knew it.

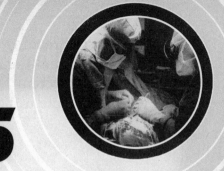

5

TEMPER, TEMPER

From the time he was eight until he was thirteen or fourteen, Ben had clung to the dream of becoming a missionary doctor. But about the time he began wanting fancy clothes, he decided he'd lived in dire poverty long enough. Instead of becoming a missionary doctor, he'd become a psychiatrist instead.

Ben didn't know any psychiatrists, but on television they all looked rich. They lived in fancy mansions, drove Jaguars, and worked in big, plush offices. And all they had to do was talk to crazy people all day long.

Since I seem to be talking to crazy people all day long already, Ben thought, *this is going to work out extremely well.*

Ben started reading *Psychology Today* magazine and began making new plans. He'd still be a doctor, just a different kind. There was, however, one major obstacle to Ben's becoming a doctor of any kind.

★

One day during the time Ben was still worried about looking cool, his mother gave him a new pair of pants. Ben looked at them and told her, "I will *not* wear those. They're the wrong kind!"

"What do you mean 'wrong kind?'" his mother asked. She had just gotten home from work and was tired. "You need new pants. Now just wear these."

"No!" Ben yelled. And he threw the pants at his mother.

Mrs. Carson quietly folded the pants and laid them across the back of a kitchen chair. "I can't take them back. They were on special."

"I don't care! I won't wear them! They're not what I want!"

"Bennie," said his mother, "we don't always get what we want."

"I will!" yelled Ben. He raised his right arm and his hand flew toward his mother. Curtis, who had been watching, grabbed Ben from behind and wrestled him away from their mother.

Ben usually was a good kid. He seldom got into trouble. But he was definitely having trouble with his temper. He didn't get angry easily, but when he did, he completely lost control. Even now, after almost hitting his mother, he didn't want to admit to himself that he had a serious problem with anger.

One day he hit a boy in the hallway at school. Because he had the lock from his locker in his hand at the time, the blow opened a three-inch gash in the other kid's forehead. Ben ended up in the principal's office. Another time Ben got angry and threw a rock at a kid, breaking the kid's glasses and bloodying his nose.

Still, each time, Ben brushed it off. *I didn't mean to hurt anyone. I'm a good kid. I can handle my temper. It's not really a problem,* he told himself.

Then one day something happened that Ben could no longer ignore. It changed Ben's life forever.

Ben was in ninth grade. He and his friend Bob were listening to the radio at Bob's house when Bob leaned over and changed the tuner to another station. Ben changed it back. Bob switched stations again. Suddenly Ben lost control. He grabbed the camping knife that he carried in his pocket, snapped the blade open, and lunged at Bob's stomach. The blade hit Bob's large metal belt buckle and broke off.

Ben was so angry he could have sliced open Bob's belly. Bob could have been lying at Ben's feet, bleeding to death. Ben could have been charged with murder and spent the rest of his teenage years in juvenile detention. But he was lucky the knife hit Bob's large metal belt buckle.

Bob looked at Ben, but was too surprised to say anything.

Ben muttered, "I ... I ... I'm sorry," then dropped the knife handle and ran for home.

There, Ben locked himself in the bathroom and sank to the floor. *I tried to kill my friend!* he thought. *I must be crazy. Only a crazy person would kill a friend.*

He squeezed his eyes shut, but that didn't keep him from seeing what had just happened, over and over again in his mind: his hand ... the knife ... the broken blade ... Bob's face. For hours Ben sat there remembering. He felt sick and miserable. Sweat dripped down his back. He was disgusted with himself.

Then he remembered to pray.

In that small bathroom, he finally realized that he had a problem with his temper. He realized he couldn't control his temper by himself. He needed help. He needed God's help.

Lord, Ben prayed, *you've got to help me. Please take this temper away!*

For about a year, Ben had been reading *Psychology Today* magazine. He had read that a person's temper is a personality trait, and that people have to accept their personality traits. Usually you cannot change them. But Ben knew that he would never achieve his dream of being a doctor if he continued to have such problems with his temper.

Lord, he persisted, *please change me. You promise in the Bible that if I ask anything in faith, you will do it. And I believe that you can change me!*

Ben slipped out of the bathroom and got a Bible to read. Back on the bathroom floor, he opened the Bible to Proverbs. The first verses he saw were about anger and how angry people have nothing but trouble. They seemed to be written just for Ben. One verse that he read over and over was Proverbs 16:32 RSV: "He who is slow to anger is better than the mighty, and he who rules his spirit than he who takes a city."

It was as if God were talking right to Ben. After he had read and prayed for a while, he was filled with a sense of peace. He stopped crying. His hands quit shaking. He knew God had answered his prayer.

He had been in that bathroom for four hours. But when he came out, he knew God had done something in his heart. He had been changed.

And Ben Carson never again had trouble with his temper.

6

DECISIONS, DECISIONS

Ben had made his decision to trust God, become a Christian, and be baptized back when he was eight years old. At the age of twelve, he had asked to be baptized again. He had told his minister, "I didn't really grasp the importance of what I was doing when I was younger. I'm twelve now. I understand and I'm ready now." So his pastor had re-baptized him.

But after Ben tried to stab his friend—after his four hours in the bathroom that day at the age of fourteen—Ben's faith became personal and heartfelt in a way it had never been before. He began reading the Bible and praying every day.

Ben also realized that he didn't need to be afraid of anything—that the same God who had changed his heart that day in the bathroom was the one who had created the universe. He realized that God was all-powerful and could do anything.

Ben's conviction that God wanted him to be a doctor became stronger than ever.

★

Ben spent the last two years of high school making up for his one year of goofing off in school—when he'd been more concerned about how to dress and act to fit in with the crowd in the school hallways than how to stand out in the classroom. He worked so hard that by the time he graduated, he had climbed back up to be ranked third academically in his senior class.

That class standing, combined with a high score on the Scholastic Aptitude Test (SAT), meant that he could go almost anywhere he wanted to go to college. He was offered a full scholarship to attend West Point. The University of Michigan pursued him, but Ben really wanted to go to a school farther from home. Representatives came from many colleges to meet with Ben and try to persuade him to attend their schools.

By the spring of his senior year of high school, he had narrowed the decision down to two schools—Harvard or Yale. But Ben didn't know how to decide between them. Clearly, either one could give him a good foundation for medical school. Both were offering him substantial scholarships.

Then one Sunday afternoon Ben was watching one of his favorite television shows: *General Electric College Bowl,* a quiz show where teams from different colleges competed against each other, answering questions about a variety of subjects. The two college teams competing that day were from Harvard and Yale.

Ben was so impressed to see the Yale students blow Harvard away, by a score of something like 510–35, that his decision was instantly sealed. Forget Harvard. Yale it would be!

★

When he walked onto that campus in the fall of 1969, he expected to impress everyone. After all, he had done great in high school and had scored high on the SAT. Months of listening to college recruiters telling him how much they wanted him to come to their schools had left Ben thinking he was pretty special. Yale, he thought, was lucky he had chosen to go there.

He had been on the campus only a week or so when he began to realize he was not the only bright student at Yale.

Ben was sitting at a table in a dining hall with some fellow students when they began comparing SAT scores. He quickly discovered that everyone at that table had scored higher than he had on the SAT. That was his first clue that college was going to be a big step up from high school.

Perhaps that should have scared Ben into working harder at his studies. But it didn't. He had always been able to read and go to classes, but not really study until right before a test. Then he would cram for a day or so and make good grades. But that familiar strategy didn't work so well for college classes at Yale.

Each day, each week of that first semester, Ben felt himself slipping farther and farther behind in his college classes. He fell so far behind that in his chemistry class, he was failing. He had, in fact, the lowest grade in the class.

The afternoon before the final exam in chemistry, Ben walked around the campus thinking and worrying as the seriousness of his situation sank in.

I am going to fail chemistry! If I fail chemistry, I won't be able to continue my pre-med studies. I'll never be a doctor. And that is all I've ever wanted to be!

He turned the matter over and over in his mind. The only hope he had was a small one: the chemistry professor had a rule. If someone was doing poorly in his class, but did very well on the final exam, the professor would toss out the other grades and use just the final exam grade. That was Ben's only chance of passing the course.

He would just have to do well on the final. *But how am I going to do that when I don't understand what we've covered?*

Decisions, Decisions

That's when Ben heard his mother's voice: *Bennie, you can do whatever you set your mind to do.*

So Ben headed back to his dorm to study. He didn't know how he could learn everything he needed to learn in order to make a good grade on the final. But he had to at least try.

Back in his room, as he opened his chemistry book, he prayed: *Lord, I need your help! I've always thought you wanted me to be a doctor. But I can't be a doctor if I fail this class. Please, either let me know what else I ought to do or perform a miracle and help me pass this exam.*

He studied for hours, memorizing formulas and equations, reading through the textbook, trying to understand what he had not been able to grasp all semester. Finally, at about midnight, his thoughts began to run together and the words on the pages blurred.

He flipped off his light and lay down on his bed. Before he drifted off to sleep, he whispered into the darkness: "God, please forgive me for failing you."

During the night, Ben had a strange dream. In that dream, he was seated in his chemistry class, the only person there. A shadowy figure walked into the front of the room and began writing chemistry problems on the board. The figure worked the problems and came up with the answers—all while Ben sat and watched.

When Ben woke up the next morning, he clearly remembered what he had seen on the board in his dream. He got up and began writing down the problems. A few of the answers were fuzzy, but he remembered the problems with a clarity that surprised him.

Then he showered, dressed, and ate breakfast. As he headed toward his chemistry final, he felt numb from exhaustion and the sure knowledge that he was unprepared for the exam.

He walked into the lecture hall. But unlike his dream, now he was not alone. Ben watched the teacher walk around the room, handing out the test booklets to all six hundred students who would be taking the test that day.

He opened his booklet. The first problem on the page was the same problem that the shadowy figure in his dream had first written on the board. Ben took a deep breath. *Was this real? Could this really be happening?* He thumbed through the test booklet to confirm what he now suspected. All the problems in the booklet were identical to the ones in his dream.

Ben's pencil flew across the page. He remembered question after question; he knew the answers. Toward the end of the exam, he missed a few, where he was beginning to forget the details of the dream. But he knew he would pass!

Ben walked out of that room and walked around the Yale campus for over an hour. "Thank you, God," he prayed. "You gave me a miracle today!"

But he also promised God that he would never again ask God to rescue him like that. Ben vowed that he would learn how to study and would work hard throughout each semester, not just at the end. And that is what he did.

From that day on, Ben was more convinced than ever that God wanted him to be a doctor.

7

CANDY AND BEN

At college, Ben learned another important lesson. Walking onto the campus of Yale University and into his dormitory, Ben was awed. His modest dorm room offered the nicest living conditions he had known in his entire life. And that was just the beginning. The skinny kid from Detroit's inner city found himself visiting the homes of his professors and fellow students who came from some of the wealthiest families in America.

He could have been envious. But instead, Ben found himself fascinated by the opportunity to observe the lifestyles of the wealthy. What he saw convinced him that what his mother had always told him and Curtis was true. Rich people were not that much different from everyone else. Great success was possible. But success wouldn't happen simply by wishing his circumstances were different. If he wanted to succeed as a doctor, he would have to work hard in his classes, developing skills that would be valuable in the world around him.

At the same time, Ben noted that wealth could also be a handicap. Many of his fellow students did not seem to appreciate the value of a dollar the way he had been taught to do. They spent money on sophisticated stereo equipment for their dorm rooms, expensive outings to New York City, and lavish dates. Money created a distraction for many students that kept them from focusing on their studies. Some flunked out of school their first year.

Seeing this, Ben realized that in one sense, his lack of money, which made him feel self-conscious at first, actually contributed to his academic success. Without the opportunities and distractions money could buy, he found it easier to keep up with his studies than many of his classmates did.

Ben met Candy Rustin just before his third year at Yale. But he was so focused on his responsibilities that he almost missed out on romance. Working hard to pay his expenses and make the best possible grades, Ben found little time for dating or even thinking about women.

But each year, Yale hosted a reception for incoming freshmen from Michigan at the Grosse Point Country Club. Upperclassmen from Michigan were on hand to welcome the new students. At that reception, Ben noticed a pretty young woman with a bubbly laugh who seemed to be talking to everyone. *That is one good-looking girl!* he thought. That afternoon was the beginning of their friendship.

Some time later, Ben saw Candy again, walking across campus. He smiled and asked how she was doing in her classes. "I think I'm making all A's," she answered. *Wow! She must be really smart,* Ben thought.

Ever since Ben's first year at Yale, he had regularly attended worship services at a nearby church. The congregation became like a second family for him. Nearly every week after services, someone would invite Ben and his roommate to eat dinner with them. Ben sang in the choir, and Aubrey Tompkins, the choir director, often gave Ben a ride to and from church.

Now, with Ben's encouragement, Candy auditioned to be the organist for that choir. She didn't get the job, but she stayed to sing in the choir.

So she and Ben would see each other around campus during the week and at church on the weekends. Before long, they both began attending a church-sponsored Bible study and meeting after classes to talk.

They were still just friends—both too busy with school to think about being anything more.

During the Thanksgiving holiday the following year, Ben and Candy were hired by the university to interview students from Michigan who had high SAT scores. Ben rented a car, and Ben and Candy drove from town to town meeting with students from the Detroit area who wanted to attend Yale. Between appointments, they spent time visiting their own friends and family.

On the last day of their holiday, Ben and Candy were late getting started back to Yale. Ben had to return the rental car by eight the next morning in New Haven. To make that deadline, they realized they would have to drive all night long.

Their route was on mostly interstate highways. But Ben was already exhausted. "I don't know if I can stay awake," he told Candy as they headed back to Connecticut.

Shortly after they crossed the state line into Ohio, Candy fell asleep. Ben let her doze, knowing that their whirlwind recruiting trip had left her tired too.

About one in the morning, Ben noticed a sign that said, "Youngstown, Ohio." The speed limit was 70 miles per hour, but Ben was cruising between 80 and 90 miles an hour. They were making good progress, and it looked like they would make it back on time.

The car felt comfortably warm. Candy slept peacefully in the passenger seat. Few vehicles shared the road at that time of morning. In fact, it had been several minutes since Ben had even seen another car.

Somewhere along the road, not long after Ben saw that Youngstown sign, he fell asleep at the wheel.

The vibration of the tires as they hit the metal illuminators separating the lanes woke Ben. But all he saw in the headlights was the blackness of a ravine ahead, dropping steeply off the side of the road, and the car was heading straight into it.

Ben took his foot off the accelerator and jerked the wheel as hard as he could to turn the car back onto the roadway. The car could have flipped. But instead it went into a spin—turning round and round in the eastbound lane of the highway.

Ben took his hands off the steering wheel as scenes of his childhood flashed through his mind. *This must be what it's like to die*, he thought.

When the car finally stopped spinning, Ben saw that they were in the far right lane of the highway—the motor still running, the car pointing in the right direction.

Shaking, Ben eased the car off the roadway and onto the shoulder of the road. A split second later, a large tractor-trailer truck barreled by.

Ben shut the motor off and sat there in the darkness. "We're alive. God saved our lives! Thank you, God," he said out loud.

Ben's voice woke Candy, who had slept through the whole incident. "Is something wrong, Ben?" she asked. "Why are we stopped here?"

"We're all right," Ben assured her.

But Candy persisted, "What's going on? Why did we stop?"

Ben started the car and began to pull back onto the road.

"Ben, please tell me," Candy persisted.

Ben pulled back off the road, took a deep breath, and told her what had happened. His heart was still racing and his voice choked up as he told her, "I thought we were both going to die."

Candy reached over and took Ben's hand. "The Lord spared us. He must have a plan for us."

After that neither Ben nor Candy could go back to sleep. They talked and drove until sunrise.

Soon after, Ben and Candy realized they were in love.

In his final year of college, like all pre-med students, Ben applied to medical schools. But unlike the other pre-med students who were worried about which medical school would accept them, Ben was confident that he would go to the University of Michigan School of Medicine. He believed so firmly that God wanted him to be a doctor that he wasn't worried that he wouldn't be accepted.

One day another student was agonizing about his own medical school applications when he turned to Ben and asked, "Carson, aren't you worried?"

"No," Ben answered. "I'm going to the University of Michigan."

"How can you be sure?" the friend demanded to know.

"Easy," replied Ben. "My Father owns the university."

Ben never did explain that the Father he was talking about was his heavenly Father, the one who created the universe and, therefore, owned everything in it, including all the universities.

And Ben was right. His application to the University of Michigan School of Medicine was accepted immediately.

Candy still had two more years at Yale, which meant they would be apart for most of the next two years. But they vowed to write to each other every single day, and the boxes of love letters they still have prove they did just that.

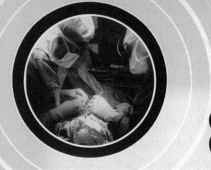

8

SUMMER JOBS

Being separated from Candy wasn't the only difficult thing about medical school. Ben's classes were harder than he ever imagined they would be.

Despite Ben's success at Yale, he really struggled his first year in medical school. His adviser felt Ben might not be smart enough to handle med school and suggested he drop out. When he refused, Ben was advised to take half as many classes. That meant Ben's medical school would take four years!

Despite the discouraging visit with his adviser, Ben knew he could do it! The key was to understand why he was struggling and come up with a strategy for solving the problem.

Ben soon realized that it was not whether he could learn—but how. His classes were all lectures, which meant six to eight hours of sitting in a class-room listening. Nothing seemed to be sinking in. He knew he had always learned best by reading, and now he needed to find a way to use that strength.

For the rest of his medical school training, Ben skipped most of his class lectures. Instead, he spent those hours, and a lot more, in his room or at the library reading. He read the textbooks. He studied all sorts of related resources. He paid other students to take notes in his classes, and he read and studied those. Plus he made sure to be in all the labs for the hands-on experiments.

Ben's new study strategy worked! His school-work was so much better that he not only shocked his adviser, he surprised himself.

But medical school was never easy for Ben. He studied so long and had so much material to cover that he often fell asleep reading his assignments. To keep himself awake, Ben tried standing up and walking around his dorm room as he read. He also learned to pace himself by reading just forty-five minutes at a time and then rewarding himself with fifteen minutes to do anything he wished.

★

During each school year throughout college and medical school, Ben made studying for classes his main job. But each summer, he worked at other jobs in order to save money for his school expenses. One summer he worked in a biology laboratory at

Wayne State University. Another summer job put him in the payroll office at the Ford Motor Company, where he wore a shirt and tie to work each day. Another summer he worked on an assembly line for Chrysler Motor Company, putting car fenders together. Another summer job was as a radiology technician, taking X rays.

For two summers, Ben held a job in highway trash collection. He supervised a crew of six guys whose job it was to walk along interstate highways picking up litter. The highway department had several such crews, and most of their workers picked up an average of two bags of trash each day. Ben knew his guys could do that much in an hour if they worked harder. But he decided they might do even better with a new approach.

Ben struck a deal with his crew. If they would come to work at six in the morning, hours ahead of the other litter crews, and collect a total of 150 bags of trash—25 bags each—they could then go home. And they would be paid for the whole day.

Ben's workers agreed to the deal and made a contest of it, competing with each other to see who could collect the most trash in the shortest amount of time. They worked in the cool of the morning and often got back to the Department of Transportation in time to see the other crews just starting to work. They laughed and teased the other crews who were headed out in the heat of the day, with long hours of work ahead of them.

Ben knew he wasn't following the instructions he'd been given for his crew. But since his crew kept setting records for the most trash collected, no one ever complained.

What Ben did not understand at that time was how finding a creative approach to this work would help him as a doctor. But one of the characteristics that would one day make him a great doctor was his ability to see new and better ways to get work done.

★

Even though he found good jobs and worked hard every summer, Ben had little money to spend during the school year. Once, when he was broke during his sophomore year, he walked across campus, thinking and praying, *Lord, please help me. I need at least enough money for bus fare to get to church!*

As Ben approached the old college chapel, he looked down and saw a ten-dollar bill lying on the ground. *Thank you, Lord!*

During his junior year, he hit the same low point—not enough money for even bus fare or a phone call. He took another walk across campus to the chapel, looking on the ground for money the entire way. But no luck.

That same day, to make matters worse, he had to retake a test. According to a notice, the exam papers from a psychology test he had taken a few days earlier had been "inadvertently burned." So Ben headed over to class to take the test again.

The professor handed out the tests to the 150 students and then left. Ben began reading the questions. *Whoa! These are much, much more difficult than the questions on the original test!*

Evidently, Ben wasn't the only person who thought so. After a moment, another student spoke up:

"Can you believe this? I can't answer these! They're too hard! I'm leaving. I'll tell the professor that I didn't see the notice about the retest. They'll have to do the test again, and I'll know what to study the next time." With that, the student got up and left the classroom. Soon other students decided to do the same thing.

Ben kept staring at the test. It wasn't fair! *But I have to try and do my best,* he thought. *I won't lie and say I didn't see the notice.*

Ben kept working, occasionally hearing other students get up and walk out. Half an hour later, he was the only student left in the room.

Suddenly, the door swung open and the professor walked in. With her was a photographer who walked over and took Ben's picture.

"What's going on?" Ben asked.

"A hoax," the professor replied. "We wanted to see who was the most honest person in this class. And you won!" Then the professor handed Ben his reward: a ten-dollar bill.

★

That summer between college and medical school, Ben could not find a job. Companies were laying people off, not hiring. His mother was caring for the children of the president of Sennet Steel. So Mrs. Carson spoke to Mr. Sennet about Ben, and he gave Ben a job at his steel company, operating a crane.

That summer Ben learned something important about himself. As a crane operator, he had to work the levers exactly right so that the boom on the crane swung over tall stacks of material, picking up the steel in such a way that it didn't tip or swing. Ben had to maneuver the steel onto trucks parked in a narrow space.

What Ben discovered was that he had an unusual ability—a gift from God—to think and see in three dimensions. He could visualize how the steel would move and where it would fit. This helped him operate the crane. It would also one day help him during surgery to see his patients in three dimensions. This gift enables him to understand what is happening in each surgery, even in the parts of the brain that he cannot actually see.

★

That special ability to see in three dimensions helped Ben come up with a new surgical technique while he was still a student in medical school.

One day Ben was watching the teacher—a neurosurgeon—perform a surgical procedure on a patient. "The hardest part is finding the foramen ovale," the surgeon told his students as they watched him probe the back of the patient's head with a long needle. The foramen ovale is the little hole at the base of the skull.

There ought to be an easier way! Ben thought. *Surely there's another approach that works better.*

After class he went to the radiology lab where he had worked one summer. His friends there let him use the equipment, and Ben began to search for a better way to perform the procedure. It took him several days, but Ben hit upon an idea to use two small metal rings and an X ray to locate the foramen ovale on patients without having to poke them again and again with a needle.

At first he didn't want to tell the doctors about his discovery. After all, he was just a medical student. They were professors and neurosurgeons with years of experience. But Ben finally had a few chances to try his technique and found out that it really worked.

When he finally showed his teachers what he had discovered, the head professor said, "That's fabulous, Carson." Soon all the doctors were using Ben's new technique.

★

In Ben's last year of medical school, he had some important decisions to make: where to do his internship and residency and what area of medicine he wanted to specialize in.

As he considered a specialty, Ben thought, *What is it that I'm really good at? I have excellent hand-eye coordination. I'm a very careful person. And I am fascinated by the human brain. I loved doing my two rotations in neurosurgery.... I believe I would make a great brain surgeon!*

There was no way that Ben Carson could imagine where that decision was about to take him.

MARANDA FRANCISCO

Having decided he wanted to specialize in neurosurgery, Ben applied to do his residency at Johns Hopkins Medical Institutions—perhaps the best and most famous training hospital in the world. The day he learned he had been accepted into Johns Hopkins' neurosurgery program was one of the happiest and most exciting days of his life.

But *the* happiest and most exciting day of Ben's life had come several years earlier—the day he and Candy were married.

Candy had just graduated from Yale, and Ben was between his second and third years of medical school. For the first few years, Ben and Candy lived in a small apartment in Ann Arbor, Michigan, while Ben finished his work at the University of Michigan Medical School.

From Ann Arbor, the young couple moved to Baltimore, Maryland, where Ben began training in neurosurgery at Johns Hopkins.

On his first day at Johns Hopkins, Ben walked toward a nurses' station wearing green scrubs. A nurse looked up at him and asked, "Whom did you come to pick up?" She obviously thought he was an orderly.

"I didn't come to pick up anyone." Ben smiled. "I'm the new intern."

The nurse stammered an apology.

"That's okay," Ben said, "I'm new, so why should you know who I am?"

After his internship, Ben was a resident at Johns Hopkins from 1978 until 1982. During that time, Ben encountered other people who were surprised to see a black doctor on the staff at the famous hospital. Once in a while, a patient would tell Dr. Long, Ben's supervisor, that they did not want to be treated by a black physician. But each time Dr. Long told them, "You are free to leave whenever you wish. But if you stay, Dr. Carson will be your doctor." No one ever walked out.

For a time, Candy worked for an insurance company, then got a job at the hospital, working as an assistant to one of the chemistry professors. Ben worked such long hours as a resident, he was seldom home. So Candy made use of the time to go back to school herself. She earned a master's degree in business administration and landed a good job at a bank.

During his residency, Ben mastered the basics of neurosurgery. He also conducted research studies and impressed his teachers with both his surgical skills and his character. By the time he completed his training, the head of his department invited him to stay and serve on the faculty. But Ben and Candy had another adventure in mind.

Ben had met a neurosurgeon who kept telling him, "You should come to Australia and be a senior *registrar* (a word meaning *surgeon* Down Under) at our teaching hospital in Perth."

At first, Ben didn't take the offer seriously. But his Australian friend kept talking, and Ben kept listening. Finally, he and Candy sensed that God was leading them to Australia. They spent every bit of their savings for two one-way airline tickets and headed for the other side of the world.

The teaching hospital where Ben worked was a major center for neurosurgery for the entire continent. In his one year in Australia, Ben was able to gain more experience in performing various techniques than some surgeons receive in a lifetime practicing in the United States.

When his year in Australia was over, Ben and Candy returned to the States. They brought with them their newborn son, Murray.

Ben was welcomed back to take his place on the faculty at Johns Hopkins. A few months later, when the position of chief of pediatric neurosurgery came open, Ben was asked to fill it. He was only thirty-three years old.

Less than a year later, Ben met a patient named Maranda Francisco. Other doctors had given this little girl and her parents no hope of recovery. But Ben decided to try a different approach to Maranda's problem.

When Ben first saw Maranda, she was having as many as a hundred seizures each day. Ben noted that the seizures always began with trembling at the right corner of Maranda's mouth. Then the right side of her face would shake. Then her right arm and right leg would begin to jerk until the whole right side of her body was moving. Finally, she would go limp.

By the time Maranda arrived at the hospital, she had almost stopped eating. It was too dangerous; she might choke. She was also forgetting how to walk and talk and needed constant supervision and a lot of medication.

For several weeks, Ben studied Maranda's records. After noting that all the seizures began on her right side, Ben determined that the cause lay somewhere in the left side of her brain. That gave him an idea. If the damaged half of her brain could be removed, the seizures would stop.

So Ben read all the articles and papers he could find about a procedure called a *hemispherectomy*, a surgery in which one entire side, or half, of a patient's brain is removed. The procedure had been attempted decades earlier—with little or no success. But technology and surgical techniques had improved greatly since then. *Maybe*, Ben thought, *just maybe the surgery could now be done successfully.*

Ben knew that Maranda's surgery would be one of the most difficult he had ever attempted. He also knew that the outcome could change his career and the attitudes of other doctors toward a controversial procedure. There were many unanswered questions.

The left half of the brain controls speech. If Ben removed it, would Maranda still be able to talk? With half of her brain gone, would she be able to see, to walk? Because the left side of her brain controls the right side of the body, would the surgery leave Maranda paralyzed on the right side? No one knew the answers to any of these questions.

What Ben did know was this: the disease that had damaged this little girl's brain was getting worse. If Ben did not operate, Maranda would die.

Finally Ben spoke with Maranda and her parents: "I am willing to do a hemispherectomy. But I have never done one before. Maranda might die on the operating table. Or we might damage the other side of her brain."

"What will happen if we don't do the surgery?" her parents asked.

"She will get worse and then die," Ben answered.

"If there is any chance," her parents said, "we want you to operate."

The evening before the surgery, Ben visited Maranda and her parents in her hospital room. He went over all the information about the procedure with them one more time. Then he told them: "I have a homework assignment for you. I give this to every patient and their family before surgery."

"Whatever you want us to do," Maranda's father said, puzzled that this doctor thought there was anything they could do.

"Say your prayers, tonight," Ben said. "I believe prayer helps."

Maranda's parents agreed.

Ben promised that he, too, would pray. And that night, before Ben went to bed, he asked God to guide his hands and give life back to Maranda Francisco.

The next day in the operating room, from the beginning things did not go well. Maranda's brain was so damaged by the seizures that wherever the doctors touched it, the tissue began to bleed. Wherever Ben cut, small blood vessels had to be sealed carefully and blood had to be suctioned away before he could see what he was doing.

Ben's surgical team included another surgeon, Dr. Neville Knuckley, as well as nurses, technicians, and anesthesiologists. The excessive bleeding kept them all busy.

Slowly, meticulously, for more than eight hours, Ben separated the left side of Maranda's brain from the right side. As he worked, Ben continued to ask God to guide his hands.

Almost ten hours after she was taken into surgery, Maranda's skull was stitched back into place, and the doctors stepped away from the table. They had successfully removed the left side of her brain. But no one yet knew what that would mean— would Maranda's seizures stop? Would she be able to speak?

As Ben followed the gurney carrying Maranda out of surgery, Maranda's parents heard them coming down the hall. Running from the waiting room to see their daughter, Mrs. Francisco leaned over and kissed her little daughter. Maranda's eyes opened slightly, and in a small voice she said, "I love you, Mommy and Daddy." The question about whether Maranda would be able to speak had been answered.

News that Maranda had survived the surgery and that she had spoken moved quickly through the hospital!

Then Maranda squirmed around a little on the gurney, moving her right arm and right leg, proving that her right side was not paralyzed! Best of all, the seizures did not return.

Maranda's surgery was the first of many hemi-spherectomies Ben Carson would perform. Many of those patients have recovered and gone on to live normal lives.

★

Since that time, Ben has seen many patients who, like Maranda, are plagued with seizures. Some are caused by brain tumors, and some are the result of accidents, birth defects, or developmental problems. Most of the children he treats are referred to Johns Hopkins by other doctors who feel they don't have enough experience to treat the conditions. For that reason, Ben sees many patients with complicated problems who are extremely ill. For a great many, he has been able to provide hope and another chance at life.

Two such patients, born in Germany in February 1987, were twin brothers—Patrick and Benjamin Binder. Though they were born on another continent, their arrival at Johns Hopkins would change Ben Carson's life every bit as much as he changed theirs.

10

PATRICK AND BENJAMIN BINDER

Patrick and Benjamin were craniopagus Siamese twins. When the boys were born, their heads were attached. Twins like this are so rare that it happens only once in every two million births. And most craniopagus Siamese twins die at birth.

Doctors do not understand completely what causes this to happen. But most believe the twins grow from one egg that doesn't completely separate. A few believe the babies separate, but then grow back together.

Patrick and Benjamin seemed to be healthy babies in every other way. Their heads were joined at the back, so they were facing away from each other. That meant they couldn't move like normal babies. As long as they remained attached, they would never be able to walk, crawl, sit, or even turn over. And they couldn't see each other.

Not long after their birth in Germany, the babies' doctor contacted Johns Hopkins to see if surgery could separate the twins. Ben looked over the boys' records and studied the available medical research. He knew the surgery would be difficult. But he also knew that surgery was Patrick's and Benjamin's only hope for normal lives.

The surgery would be a challenge—the challenge of a lifetime, a type of surgery Ben could expect to perform only once. It would require seventy medical personnel: seven pediatric anesthesiologists; five neurosurgeons; two cardiac surgeons; five plastic surgeons, and dozens of nurses and technicians.

Ben and three other doctors who would be involved, Craig Dufresne, Mark Rogers, and David Nichols, planned to fly to Germany to examine the boys and meet their parents. While there, Dr. Dufresne would insert balloons under the twins' scalps to help stretch the skin. The extra skin would be needed to cover the boys' skulls after they were separated. To grow that much skin would take several months.

But the unexpected happened. Just two weeks before Ben was scheduled to fly to Germany, the Carsons' house was broken into. One of the things stolen was Ben's passport. He couldn't go overseas without it.

Ben asked the police investigating the break-in if they thought he might get his papers back.

"No chance," the police responded. "The thieves will just throw them away."

Ben called the passport office. "I'm sorry, Dr. Carson," he was told. "We can't replace your passport in such a short time."

So Ben prayed, "Lord, if you want me to help with this surgery, you'll have to help me get another passport."

Two days later, the police called. A detective had found Ben's passport—and other stolen documents—in a garbage container. Ben was able to go to Germany to examine the twins after all.

The surgical team at Johns Hopkins spent the next five months getting ready for the separation. They had five three-hour dress rehearsals, during which they practiced the procedure with life-sized dolls attached with Velcro. After each practice round, the medical personnel would discuss the procedure in detail, trying to anticipate anything that could go wrong and how it should be handled. They even determined where each person would stand so they wouldn't get in each other's way.

The doctors' plan was to use a combination of hypothermia, circulatory bypass, and deliberate cardiac arrest. The babies' temperatures would be lowered in order to slow their bodily functions. A bypass would circulate the boys' blood through a heart-lung machine. And doctors also decided to intentionally stop the boys' hearts from beating. Never before had all three techniques been used at the same time. But the doctors believed the use of all three was the best way to prevent brain damage.

Finally, on September 5, 1987, at 7:15 in the morning, the doctors began the surgery to separate the seven-month-old twins.

The anesthesiologists gave the babies medicine so they would sleep through the surgery. The heart surgeons inserted monitors to keep track of how well the boys' hearts were doing.

Next, Ben carefully began the incisions into the babies' scalp. He cut away an area of the skull, preserving the bony tissue so it could be used to shape and rebuild the boys' skulls.

The doctors could then work on the dura, the tough membrane that covers the brain. This had many irregularities that Ben and the other doctors had to work around. Slowly and carefully they began to snip and cut away at the places where the two boys were joined.

After a time the doctors came to the part of the boys' brains called the *torqula*. The twins shared a single torqula that was much larger than normal. And when Ben started to cut into it in order to divide the joined torqula, the babies began to bleed badly.

To keep the boys from bleeding, doctors quickly decided to go ahead and put the twins into hypothermic arrest. They hooked the boys up to a heart-lung machine that chilled their blood, bringing their temperature down from 95 degrees Fahrenheit to 68 degrees Fahrenheit. They also stopped the hearts of both boys and turned off the heart-lung machines, stopping blood from flowing into the babies' bodies. This allowed the doctors to separate the brains of both boys and rebuild the twins' blood vessels without the boys bleeding to death.

But they could leave the babies in hypothermic arrest for only one hour. After that, brain damage would occur if the machines were not turned back on to circulate warmed blood back through the babies' bodies.

Everyone in the room understood the surgery was now a life-and-death race against the clock. They had only one hour to separate the boys.

The room was quiet as everyone worked together, each doing their part. Twenty minutes later, Ben cut the final blood vessel that connected the two boys. For the first time in their lives, Patrick and Benjamin Binder were individuals—completely separate individuals.

Ben Carson took over the surgery on one baby, and Dr. Donlin Long took over on the other. They had forty minutes left to rebuild all the separate blood vessels for each child so blood could flow through them. Doctors had thought this part of the surgery would take almost an hour—too long.

To save time, the heart surgeons looked over the shoulders of Dr. Carson and Dr. Long to see what sizes and shapes of replacement tissue would be needed. They cut pieces to match and did such a good job that Ben and Dr. Long were able to work much faster.

Dr. Long finished his twin first. Ben finished his baby with only seconds to spare.

"It's done!" someone said. The heart-lung machines were turned back on and the babies' blood began to flow again. But the danger wasn't over.

For the next three hours, the doctors fought to control the bleeding from small blood vessels that had been cut during the surgery. Because the blood had to be thinned to run it through the heart-lung machine, now that thinned blood wouldn't clot. Every blood vessel that could bleed did bleed.

The surgical team tied off or joined the ends of the tiny blood vessels as fast as they could. To replace the blood the boys were losing, doctors kept giving the babies more and more blood.

Finally, there was no more blood. The hospital blood bank was out. Calls were made all over Baltimore, and the proper blood type was finally located at the Red Cross Blood Bank. They had ten pints, which turned out to be exactly what the surgeons needed to finish the surgery.

But even after the doctors got the bleeding under control, there was no time to celebrate. The twins' brains were beginning to swell so fast Ben was afraid the surgeons wouldn't be able to get the scalps closed. So they gave the boys a drug to put them into a coma and slow down their brain activity. Finally, Ben and the other neurosurgeon stepped back and let the plastic surgeons piece the skulls back together and cover the bone with the scalp tissue.

Twenty-two hours after the surgery began, the team walked out of the operating room. One of the staff doctors went to the twins' mother and, with a smile on his face, asked, "Which child would you like to see first?"

Ben knew the surgery was just the first step. While it was a giant step, the twins still had a long road of recovery ahead. So he began to pray, *Oh, God, let both boys live. Let them make it!*

Patrick and Benjamin Binder remained in a coma for ten days. During that time, their parents and doctors could only wait and hope . . . and pray. Would the boys wake up? Would they be able to live a normal life? Ben kept telling himself, *It's all in God's hands. That's where it's always been.*

One day in the middle of the second week, Ben stopped by to check on the twins. "They're moving!" he said. "Look! He moved his left foot. See?"

Later that day, both boys opened their eyes and started looking around. "He can see! They both can see! He's looking at me!" someone exclaimed.

"Thank you, thank you!" Ben told God again and again.

A few months later Theresa and Franz Binder went home to Germany with their beloved twin boys. But by then the publicity surrounding the case had made Ben something of a celebrity. He began to receive referrals from doctors around the country and around the world. He was also in great demand as a speaker, telling his story to all kinds of audiences—young and old.

THE MAKWAEBA
TWINS—WHY?

Ben had thought the Binder surgery was a once-in-a-lifetime case. But he was wrong. Seven years after the surgery on the Binder twins, Ben was given a second opportunity to operate on craniopagus Siamese twins.

In January 1994, he received a phone call at work. A man said, "My name is Doctor Samuel Mokgokong. I am professor of neurosurgery at the Medical University of South Africa at Medunsa."

"How may I help you?" Ben asked.

Dr. Mokgokong explained that he was caring for a set of South African Siamese twins whose case seemed similar to that of the Binder twins.

He was hoping Ben would be willing to help in the separation of the two little girls who were his patients.

Less than a month later, Dr. Mokgokong came to the United States and brought all the necessary records for Ben to review. The twins were named Nthabiseng and Mahlatse Makwaeba, and though they were smaller than the Binders had been, they seemed to have about the same degree of attachment at the back of their heads. Ben believed there was a fair chance both girls could be saved.

But when Dr. Mokgokong asked if Ben could go to Medunsa to lead the surgical team, Ben knew the circumstances were different. The surgery on the Binder twins had taken months of careful planning. The surgical team had been made up of the finest medical personnel Johns Hopkins had to offer, doctors Ben was used to working with. In Medunsa, he would be operating with doctors he hardly knew.

There was another problem. Johns Hopkins Hospital is one of the best medical facilities in America. Would a hospital in Medunsa, South Africa, have all that would be needed to pull off such a procedure? Did they even have all the necessary equipment? Such a surgery had never before been attempted on the continent of Africa.

As Ben prayed about his decision, he remembered the Binder twins. Their surgery had catapulted him to surprising prominence as a surgeon. It had opened doors throughout the world medical community. It had led to opportunities Ben had never dreamed possible. He had been invited to speak to audiences he would not have been able to reach before.

When he thought about all the things that had happened because of the Binder twins' surgery, he wondered, *Did God want to use another pair of Siamese twins to change a country like South Africa?*

Ben could hardly wait to see what would happen on his trip to Medunsa. He sent Dr. Mokgokong home with a list of equipment that would be needed for the operation and suggestions for the fifty to sixty doctors, nurses, and technicians they would need.

When Ben arrived in South Africa, Dr. Mokgokong met his flight with bad news. The twins were sick—too sick, he believed, to undergo the surgery. When Ben examined the Makwaeba sisters, he agreed. A couple of months would be needed to give the girls a chance to regain their strength.

But Ben's visit gave him a chance to meet the surgical team and discuss strategies with them face-to-face. Ben also got a firsthand look at the facilities in Medunsa. They were very different from those in American medical schools.

The patients were cared for in large, open-air wards with twenty to thirty beds each. The windows were open, and breezes carried in whatever was in the air outside—dust, leaves, pollen, and, occasionally, flying or crawling bugs.

As Ben walked about in the hospital, he also saw doctors and nurses caring for their patients. He was impressed with the good health care they were providing.

Ben returned home sooner than he had planned, but with a greater sense of confidence. The procedure was rescheduled for June.

While Ben waited for the chance to return to South Africa, he received another honor. Each year, *Essence* magazine gave the Essence Award to African-American women they judged to have made a significant and notable contribution to the world. In 1994, for the first time, African-American men would also receive the prestigious Essence Award. Ben was one of the men chosen.

He and Candy flew to New York City, where Ben was to receive the award. As he looked around at the well-known crowd, he saw the Rev. Jesse Jackson, movie director Spike Lee, actor Denzel Washington, and comedian Eddie Murphy. They all were being honored. Ben realized he probably would not be sitting there if not for his involvement in the separation of the Binder twins back in 1987.

When June came and Ben traveled back to South Africa, he faced a difficult decision. Unfortunately, the Makwaeba twins were even sicker than they had been in April. The girls' hearts were getting so weak that the surgery seemed to be their only hope. If they weren't separated soon, they would surely die.

The doctors gathered the whole medical team together and informed them of the intention to proceed. Everyone knew the girls were not doing well. To make things even more tense, an American network television camera crew had arrived to record the whole procedure.

Like the surgery on the Binder twins, this operation required several neurosurgeons, heart surgeons, plastic surgeons, and a host of nurses and technicians. The operating rooms had brand-new ventilators, many new surgical tools, plus state-of-the-art monitors for the anesthesiologists and the cardiovascular surgeons.

The surgical tables were set up so that they could be pulled apart at the moment of separation. Then two different teams would quickly surround the individual twins to close their skulls and scalps. Remembering the rather frightening situation that had occurred during the operation on the Binder twins, Ben had the hospital stockpile a large supply of blood.

The operation began with the plastic surgeons carefully removing the scalp expanders they had put in place months earlier. When they finished, the neurosurgical team went to work.

When Ben cut through the skull, the bone proved to be unusually bloody. So he spent a lot of time trying to control the blood loss. After the fused sections of skull had been cut away, Ben could see that the underlying dura (the thick, leather-like membrane that surrounds the brain itself) was complexly connected between the twins. It had to be carefully cut and separated.

The doctors found large pools of blood called "venous lakes" and a large number of blood vessels connecting the two brains. More than a dozen hours into the surgery, it became obvious that the doctors needed to hook the twins up to a heart-lung bypass machine that would slowly drain and cool their blood to bring the babies' bodily functions to a near halt. That way, the hearts would stop pumping and the blood would stop flowing. As before, the team had only one hour after the hearts were stopped to complete their work before brain damage would occur.

Within that hour, the doctors had to separate all those interwoven blood vessels. They quickly sorted out all the connections and carefully divided the shared blood vessels before the time was up. But as soon as they began pumping blood back in the babies, the smaller twin died. Her tiny heart did not begin beating. It couldn't pump any blood at all. The surgery had lasted for fifteen hours.

Now all the doctors, as a team, concentrated on the other girl. A few hours later, when they completed the operation, she seemed in pretty good condition. She even moved a little in the recovery room. While Ben was sad about the death of the one child, everyone was glad the second twin had been saved.

A few hours after surgery, the second girl began having seizures, and her condition steadily worsened. She died two days later.

When the doctors examined her body, they found that her kidneys had stopped working. They learned that the girls had been entirely symbiotic—they depended completely on each other for life. The smaller child had relied on the larger girl's heart, and the larger girl needed her smaller sister's kidneys. If they had remained together, both the heart and the kidneys would have soon failed. The girls would have died anyway.

But that knowledge wasn't much comfort for the family or the doctors.

On the morning before he left for home, Ben was interviewed on a news show, *Good Morning, South Africa*. He tried to explain what had happened, to let people know that no hospital in the world would have been able to save the two little girls. But he felt discouraged. He had hoped and prayed for these children. He had believed that God would work a miracle. But the girls had died.

As the plane lifted off the ground in South Africa, taking Ben back home, Ben prayed: *God, why did you get me involved in a situation like this where there was never any possibility for success? Why did you let me spend so much valuable time and energy in something that could not possibly work out? Why would you provide an opportunity like this only to allow us to fail? Why?*

None of it made sense.

12

ANOTHER SET OF
TWINS—FROM ZAMBIA

For the next two and a half years, Ben continued to wonder why.

Then in December 1996, Dr. Sam Mokgokong contacted him again. The Medical University of South Africa at Medunsa wanted to present Ben with an honorary doctorate. Ben and Candy planned to fly to South Africa to receive the honor the following June.

Then that spring, Dr. Mokgokong called again. Another set of craniopagus Siamese twins had been born recently in Zambia. The doctors there had contacted Dr. Mokgokong to ask about the possibility of separating Joseph and Luka Banda. Dr. Mokgokong had flown to Zambia to examine the twins himself, and he felt they were good prospects for a successful separation.

Dr. Mokgokong also told Ben, "The Zambian government would like you and your wife to come to their country while you are in Africa so that you can examine these twins and see if you think they are candidates for surgery."

So Ben and Candy made arrangements to go to Zambia after leaving South Africa. And Ben began to think, *This is amazing. Yet another set of craniopagus Siamese twins! Less than ten years after the Binder twins!*

Dr. Mokgokong took Ben and Candy on a quick tour of the hospital and introduced them to old and new friends. Ben realized things had changed since his last visit. Dr. Mokgokong proudly told them about the many lives saved by the equipment the hospital had acquired for the failed surgery on the little girls. Ben was reminded once again that God is able to take even sad experiences and use them for good.

Ben had already received eighteen honorary degrees from other colleges and universities. But he was proud and honored that the Medical University of South Africa at Medunsa awarded him a Doctor of Medical Science.

From the time Candy and Ben began planning this trip, they had anticipated a second highlight of their visit to South Africa. They would go on a safari at Krueger National Park, a day's drive north of Medunsa.

The night before the safari, Ben prayed. He reminded God that he and Candy had only one day to visit the park. And Ben told the Lord that he would be grateful if they could see a lot of wildlife in the short time they were there. Ben never dreamed just how literally that prayer would be answered.

During the safari, their group saw all the animals they had hoped and expected to see: lions, elephants, giraffes, zebras, and many more. They even spotted rare species such as green mambas and black mambas. Their guide told them he couldn't remember ever having another single day like it. He said he saw things he had witnessed only a few times in all his years of working in the park.

At one point, the guide pulled their four-wheel-drive Land Rover to a halt right in the middle of a roaming troop of baboons.

Looking around at the fascinating but loud and rowdy creatures surrounding them, Ben recalled a television special he had seen about baboons. Ben had learned that an adult baboon's jaws were powerful enough to bite through a human skull. And Ben knew how strong a human skull was!

Ben calmly asked the driver if they really should stop right there. The guide smiled and confidently told the group that these wild animals would never bother them.

Someone had evidently forgotten to tell that to the animals. Suddenly, the entire troop of baboons began climbing onto the all-terrain vehicle. A couple of the bolder ones scrambled up on the roof and right into the Land Rover.

Fortunately, a very quick-thinking Dr. Mokgokong tossed out several slices of sandwich bread he had brought along for a picnic. As the baboons leaped away from the vehicle to grab this free snack, the guide sped away to safety.

When Ben and Candy arrived in Zambia, Dr. T. K. Lambart, that country's only neurosurgeon, met them at the airport and drove them to the children's hospital to meet Joseph and Luka Banda.

Like the Binder twins, Joseph and Luka appeared to be healthy—a promising sign. Doctors had tested them to make certain both boys had functioning hearts, lungs, stomachs, livers, and kidneys. Unlike the South African girls, all the boys' major systems seemed to work normally and independently.

Joseph and Luka had been eating well and developing right on schedule. They could cry and smile and reach out to grasp nearby objects. They kicked and squirmed with energy and enthusiasm. They would certainly have rolled over if only they could have turned in the same direction at the exact same time.

These little boys had only one significant problem. They were attached to each other at the top of their heads.

Ben looked at the way their heads were joined and wondered: *How much have their two brains been pressed together? How much are they interconnected?* He carefully examined the twins' heads, feeling along the length of their skulls' junction. He tried to imagine what problems he and the other surgeons would find inside. Then, while turning the boys gently back and forth, Ben thought of a way to answer some of his questions before he did the surgery.

Months earlier some researchers from the Johns Hopkins radiology department had invited Ben to their laboratory for a fascinating demonstration. Working with researchers from the Medical University of Singapore, they were developing a three-dimensional visual-imaging system. They hoped the program could be used by surgeons to practice virtual-reality operations on their computers.

After the researchers had demonstrated the idea, they asked Ben for suggestions. Ben had told them he would think about it. Now, months later, in a hospital on another continent, Ben saw a way to use the technology.

During the next few months, Dr. Lambart and Dr. Mokgokong gathered all the data needed: CAT scans, angiograms, and MRIs. The researchers fed the information into their computers. Then at Johns Hopkins in Baltimore, Ben was able to put on a special pair of 3-D glasses and practice the surgery on the two babies in Zambia. This new technology enabled Ben to "see" inside the heads of two little Siamese twins who were actually lying in a hospital on another continent.

He could see and study the twins' brains before he actually cut into the scalp and began the procedure in the operating room. He could spot danger areas in advance.

With the Binder twins and the Makwaeba twins, the worst part of the surgery had been sorting out the overlapping and interconnected blood vessels. Ben had to slowly and carefully separate and close off each tiny vein. Being able to see and study the blood vessels ahead of time was an incredible advantage.

★

When Ben boarded the plane to South Africa in December 1997, he felt confident. He had planned the surgery for six months. And the Banda twins had grown stronger and were now in Medunsa.

On the plane, Ben reviewed the case notes one more time. Then he leaned his head back and prayed. He had done everything he could do.

Ben arrived in South Africa late Sunday afternoon. Dr. Mokgokong met his flight and took Ben right to the hospital where they examined their young patients and spoke to their mother.

Most of the next day, December 29, Ben was busy meeting and getting acquainted with the surgical team. Several of them had participated in the unsuccessful surgery on the Makwaeba girls back in 1994. The doctors and nurses reviewed the Banda case together.

That night Ben spent a long time in personal meditation and prayer. He thanked God for the blessings of that day and asked for strength and wisdom for what was to come.

He had told Luka's and Joseph's mother, "If you will say your prayers tonight, and you ask your families and everyone you know to pray, I promise I will say mine. And then none of us will have to worry as much tomorrow."

So for several hours that night, Ben prayed for the twins. Then he looked over the angiograms (a visualization of the blood vessels after injection with a radioactive substance) one last time. The Banda babies shared a large, abnormal sinus. The surgical team had planned to give that entire sinus to one of the twins. But after praying about it, Ben decided to divide it in the middle and give half to each twin even though he knew that approach might cause more swelling, bleeding, and perhaps even death.

The surgery on the Binder babies had required a great deal of blood. And the surgery on the Makwaeba sisters had taken even more. If he split the sinus, that might cause even more bleeding and the need for yet more blood.

Still, Ben was strongly convinced that he should try to divide the shared sinus along the midpoint. But he wondered, *What will happen if I take a chance on this new, untried strategy?*

13

AN IMPOSSIBLE
OPERATION

The next day, Ben and Dr. Mokgokong arrived in the operating room before dawn. The rest of the medical team was already there. They had a pre-operation prayer meeting under a large banner that stretched across one wall declaring, "GOD BLESS JOSEPH AND LUKA." They even sang gospel songs.

When the prayer meeting ended, everyone got busy. The babies were prepped, draped, positioned, and anesthetized. Then the plastic surgeons spent a lot of time practicing the turning of the twins back and forth from one side to the other.

The surgery itself began at 6:30 A.M. Someone turned on a stereo, playing the classical music Ben had requested. Activity quieted down.

The plastic surgeons removed the scalp expanders and stretched the excess skin back. The four neurosurgeons surrounded the operating table. Ben asked Dr. Lambart, the Zambian neurosurgeon and the boys' primary doctor, if he would like to drill the first burr hole.

Then Ben used ronjeurs—a special type of clipper—to begin snipping away the bone. He proceeded very slowly. Others controlled the bleeding by carefully treating all the raw bone edges with purified beeswax.

As a result of his practice with virtual-reality surgery, Ben already knew how the two boys' brains came together. Using scissors, he cut through the dura, the membrane covering the brains. This part of the surgery took several hours. Ben carefully cut the many blood vessels, all in the right order, stopping to control the bleeding as he worked.

As each blood vessel was cut, the doctors took great care to watch the brains and look for swelling. At one point in the surgery, the doctors encountered a group of blood vessels that looked like a huge tangled ball of spaghetti. They decided to leave that challenge until later.

The neurosurgeons sewed the skin flap closed over the area. Then the plastic surgeons turned the babies over. They had to prepare the skin and drape the twins again so that the doctors could begin the same procedure on the opposite side.

While that was being done, the neurosurgeons had time to sit down in a nearby room and eat. As they ate, they watched what was happening in the operating room via closed-circuit video. They also discussed what they had done so far and agreed on what to do next. Dr. Mokgokong said to Ben, "I cannot believe how meticulous you are with each blood vessel." But Ben believed such care was important. Remarkably, there had been little blood loss so far.

The doctors spent all afternoon and into the evening repeating what they had already done on the other side of the boys' heads. The major difference on this side was the abnormal sinus Ben had prayed about the night before. But he went ahead with the unusual approach he had decided on earlier. He used clips to pinch the sinus closed. That helped control the bleeding. He cut the sinus along the midline.

The clips held, and bleeding remained minimal over the next few hours. That part of the surgery went better than anyone had expected.

Finally, Ben was ready to tackle a second area that looked like a *small* pile of spaghetti. It took several more hours to separate those entangled blood vessels. But when that was finished, the second side was complete.

It was time to go back to the first side and the larger pile of spaghetti-like blood vessels. But there was a problem. The surgeons now were more tired than they had been when they had first looked at the area.

Ben felt exhausted and discouraged. He had been operating for nineteen hours. At home in the operating room at Johns Hopkins, Ben would have used a powerful, $350,000 operating microscope to see the tiny blood vessels. All he had at Medunsa was a simple pair of loop magnifying glasses and his headlight.

Ben needed a break. While the plastic surgery team rotated the boys one more time so Ben could do the next step from a different angle, Ben collapsed in a chair in a conference room. He called in all of the medical personnel who weren't needed in the operating room. They discussed the operation and shared ideas. Everyone looked defeated.

"Perhaps we should consider stopping the operation at this point," Ben said. He wondered if they should close the wounds and give the boys and the medical team a chance to recover and regain the strength needed to go on.

"What do you think?" he asked.

Everyone agreed about what they should do—and that was to *not* stop. They told Ben they didn't think they could keep the boys alive just partially separated. They had to go on or the boys would die.

As they walked back down the hall to the operating room, Ben prayed desperately, *God, please take over and simply use me to accomplish what only you can do.*

Ben recalled two Bible verses he had read just the night before. In John 14:12–13, Jesus made a promise to his followers, "I tell you the truth, anyone who has faith in me will do what I have been doing. He will do even greater things than these, because I am going to the Father. And I will do whatever you ask in my name, so that the Son may bring glory to the Father."

So Ben stood over those babies on the operating table and prayed in Jesus' name that God would simply take over the operation. He kept praying as he began to work on the large "pile of spaghetti."

Ben's hands were now steady. He felt calm—almost as if he were just watching his hands move and someone else had actually taken over the surgery.

One after another, more than a hundred interconnected veins were isolated, separated, clipped off and/or reconnected. When Ben separated the last vein connecting Joseph and Luka, the stereo system began playing the "Hallelujah Chorus" from Handel's *Messiah*. Everyone in the operating room knew that something remarkable had just taken place.

Twenty-five hours of surgery had passed. But there was still no time to relax. Now the surgical tables were quickly pulled apart, and the doctors immediately divided into two teams of surgeons—one for each twin.

They still had a lot of work to do. And all of the neurosurgeons, despite their fatigue, were absolutely jubilant. Neither brain exhibited any serious swelling and, remarkably, there had been little blood loss. They had used less than four units of blood for the entire operation.

Even more encouraging, they saw no swelling of any of the blood vessels. That meant circulation in both brains had been successfully restored and appropriate new pathways had clearly formed. There seemed to be every reason to believe Joseph and Luka had not only survived the surgery but that both boys might actually wake up to live full and completely normal lives.

Everyone was excited as they finished their work. When all was finally done, the neurosurgeons retreated once more to the conference room where, even before the plastic surgeons closed the scalps, they fell fast asleep sitting in chairs.

After the plastic surgeons completed their work, Ben returned to the operating room. As he looked at the twins, one opened his eyes and gripped his endotracheal tube with both hands—trying to pull it out of his throat. By the time the boys reached the intensive care unit, the other twin was doing the same thing. After twenty-eight hours of surgery, this was astounding!

Congratulatory phone calls from all over the country flooded the hospital switchboard. The entire surgical team had to be escorted across the campus for a hastily called press conference. The outdoor courtyards were packed with students and hospital staff singing and dancing in a massive celebration of joy. Everyone wanted to shake the doctors' hands or pat their backs.

The press conference was jammed with television and radio reporters who had been at the hospital covering the story since the surgery began the previous morning. They had been filing hourly updates to their stations throughout the country. The story of the Banda boys had fascinated everyone in South Africa. Now it seemed as though the entire country wanted to celebrate the wonderful accomplishment.

Ben spent a few minutes answering reporters' questions, after which the other doctors took a turn. Hospital officials made official statements. The boys' mother—now a very happy woman— even made an appearance.

The Zambian ambassador delivered his country's official thanks to everyone involved, stating that the Zambian people, along with the president and first lady, had all been praying. He invited Ben and the other surgeons to a thanksgiving dinner celebration the next day in the Zambian embassy.

Unfortunately, Ben's flight home was scheduled to leave later that evening. He expected to be home in Maryland by the time the Zambian ambassador served the main course. Ben hated to miss the celebration, but in truth he was looking forward to collapsing in his own bed.

When Dr. Mokgokong dropped him off at his hotel, Ben noticed that something was wrong—the hotel was dark, and no one seemed to be inside. He rang the bell at the front desk and waited. Nothing happened.

Suddenly, a policewoman appeared at the front door. When she spotted Ben inside, she was surprised. "How did you get in?" she wanted to know.

"I walked in the front door," Ben told her. "I'm a guest here."

"That's impossible," she said, looking at Ben suspiciously. "The hotel is closed for the holiday."

"Closed? I didn't know," Ben said. "I left early yesterday morning and didn't return last night. I've been in surgery for twenty-eight hours, and I just want to get a little sleep. I need to at least get into my room to collect my luggage. I have to catch a flight out of the country tonight."

The officer smiled broadly and said, "You're that American doctor who operated on the Siamese twins, aren't you?" By the time Ben began to nod, she was shaking his hand, and then quickly called the hotel's owner. He rushed over, reopened the hotel, gave Ben his room key, and graciously promised to personally see that no one disturbed him until he needed to leave for the airport.

A couple of weeks after returning home, Ben received word that the Banda boys were amazing their doctors. They were already beginning to crawl, an activity that had been physically impossible before the surgery. Ben knew then that those two little boys were on their way to full and normal lives.

14

THINKING BIG

Almost every week, Ben travels somewhere to speak. He is such a popular speaker that people have to invite him months and sometimes years in advance. He has spoken in schools, at business conventions, in church worship services, and at the National Prayer Breakfast in Washington, D.C., where he addressed the president and most of Congress. But Ben's favorite audiences are young people.

Many Monday mornings during the school year, he hosts seven hundred to eight hundred students from Baltimore area schools who visit Johns Hopkins on educational field trips. Ben meets with them in the medical school's Turner Auditorium, where he shows them slides about neurosurgery, Siamese twins, and some of the other things that take place at Johns Hopkins.

He tries to inspire students by talking about the amazing potential of the human brain. And he always shares his own story about how reading and education turned his life around, provided an escape from poverty, and enabled his own dreams to come true.

He tells students that it doesn't matter who they are, what color their skin is, where they come from, or how much money their family has. Education is the great equalizer. For example, to become a licensed physician he needed one thing— the required education. It didn't matter that his family was poor. Education and determination were all he needed to fulfill his dream of becoming a doctor.

Whenever Ben talks to young people, he introduces himself as the director of pediatric neurosurgery at one of the greatest medical institutions in the world . . . and a former "class dummy." He points to himself as living proof that with education and God's help, anything is possible. And he challenges his listeners to "think big." That is, he says, his philosophy for success in life.

Ben Carson often uses the letters in the words THINK BIG to make a point in his speeches:

"The T is for talent," he tells them, "which God gives to every individual. Not just the ability to sing and dance and throw a ball. Very few people are talented at basketball. Only seven out of every million basketball players are good enough to play in the NBA. But all of us are good at something. We just have to think about it and ask ourselves these questions: What have I done well so far in life? What school subjects am I good at? What do I do that other people compliment me for? What do I think is fun to do that my friends think is work?

"These are your talents. When I was deciding what to do with my life, I had to spend time analyzing myself. I asked myself, *What is it that I really ought to be doing? What am I really good at?* That's how I came up with the idea to go into neurosurgery."

"The H—in THINK BIG—is for honesty. One of my classmates at Yale graduated magna cum laude. That means he made very, very high grades. But he was not honest. He often broke rules. And he cheated on exams. Our tests were based on the honor code. The professors would hand out the examinations and then leave the room. They trusted that we would not look up the answers in our books. But during exams, I often saw this student open his book. He must have thought, *The professor isn't here to see me. The other students can see me cheat, but they don't matter.* But honesty does matter. Of all my fellow classmates, he was the one who was not accepted into medical school.

"The I is for insight, which comes in part from listening to those people who have already been where you are trying to go. Solomon, the wisest man who ever lived, said, 'Wise is the man who can learn from someone else's triumphs and mistakes. The person who cannot is a fool.'

"When I was growing up, my mother worked in the homes of wealthy families. As she went about her work, Mother asked questions. She noticed what they read, how they spent their time, the kinds of activities they chose. She noticed, for example, that wealthy people did not spend much time watching television. And she gained insight from that.

"The N—in THINK BIG—is for nice. Be nice to people. Once they get over their suspicions about why you're being nice, they'll almost always be nice to you. And you can get so much more done when people are being nice to you and you're nice to them.

"If you're not a nice person, I challenge you to try it for one week. What will that mean? It means not talking about people behind their backs. I know that's going to be hard for some people. It means not talking about people in front of their back. That means if you see somebody struggling with something, help them with it. It requires putting yourself in the other person's place before you begin to criticize.

"If the elevator door is open and there is only one space left, let someone else get on. It means greeting people. When you get in the elevator say, 'Good morning.' Once people get over their initial shock, most people will be happy to talk to you. You'll find that being nice is often contagious.

"The K is for knowledge, which can make you into a more valuable person. Yes, I do have a big house. I drive nice cars. I have many of the things that money can buy. But are they important? Of course not. If somebody comes along and takes it all away, it's no big deal. I can get it all back almost immediately using what's inside my head.

"That's what Solomon meant when he said, 'Gold is nice, silver is nice, rubies are nice. But to be treasured far above all those things are knowledge, wisdom, and understanding.' Because with knowledge, wisdom, and understanding, you can get all the gold, silver, and rubies you want. But more importantly, you come to realize that gold and silver and rubies aren't really very important. It's a far more valuable thing to develop your God-given talents to the point where you become a blessing to the people around you.

"The B is for books—an invaluable resource for obtaining success. My own story is one of the best examples I could give you.

"The second I is for in-depth learning—learning for the sake of knowledge and understanding as opposed to superficial, or shallow, learning. Superficial learners are people who cram, cram, cram before a test. They may do fine on the exam, but three weeks later, they don't remember anything.

"The last letter is G—for God. We live in a society where people are always saying, 'You can't talk about God in public.' As if somehow doing so violates the concept of church and state.

"Thomas Jefferson, one of our founding fathers, had 190 religious volumes in his library. The Declaration of Independence talks about certain inalienable rights, which our Creator endows us with. The Pledge of Allegiance to our flag says we are 'one country, under God.' Almost every court-room in the land has on its walls, 'In God We Trust.' Every coin in our pockets, every bill in our wallets, also says, 'In God We Trust.'

"If it's in our Declaration of Independence, if it's in our Pledge, if it's in our courts, and it's on our money, we can certainly talk about it in public!

"We need to make it clear to people that it's all right to live by godly principles—loving our fel-lowman, caring for our neighbors, and living a life of service by developing our God-given talents so that we might be of value to the people around us. We need to remind each other there is nothing judgmental about having values and principles, and there's nothing wrong with standing for some-thing.

"If we apply these truths to our own lives, if we instill these values in the next generation, then, and only then, will America be truly united and become the greatest nation the world has ever known."

★

Whenever he tells his own story and especially when he talks about the many amazing surgeries he's been involved with, Ben makes a point of saying:

"I know God had a hand in all these events, just as I know he has had a hand in shaping everything good in my life. Thanks to God and a courageous mother, a poor kid from the streets of Detroit has been able to take part in medical miracles. I have been blessed with a wonderful wife, three healthy boys, and a loving community of church friends.

"But I want God to continue to use me to help others. So I pray that I can be the best father and husband possible and a caring member of my church and community.

"I feel an obligation to act as a role model for young people who feel trapped by their dismal situations. If I can't do anything else, I want to provide one living example of someone who came from a disadvantaged background and made it. Because I want other young people to realize that when you THINK BIG and ask God for his help in your life, dreams can come true.

We want to hear from you. Please send your comments about this
book to us in care of the address below. Thank you.

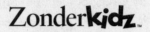

Grand Rapids, MI 49530
www.zonderkidz.com